D0516500

The Rockabilly Goats Gruff

by Jeff Crosby

Holiday House / New York

For the coolest kid I know, Harper

Special thanks to my rockin' wife, Shelley Ann Jackson;
my rollin'agent, Scott Treimel; and my souped-up critique groups:
The White Binders and the Armadillustrators.
All their patience, guidance, and honest opinions
made this book possible.

Printed and Bound in November 2013 at Kwong Fat Offset Printing Co., Ltd., DongGuan City, China.
The artwork was created with acrylics, watercolors, and water soluble crayons on watercolor paper.
www.holidayhouse.com
First Edition
1 3 5 7 9 10 8 6 4 2

Library of Congress Cataloging-in-Publication Data
Crosby, Jeff.
The rockabilly goats Gruff / by Jeff Crosby. — 1st ed.
p. cm.
Summary: Three billy goats outwit a troll that lives under the bridge they must cross
on their way to Nanny May's Shimmy Shack.
ISBN 978-0-8234-2666-9 (hardcover)
[1. Fairy tales. 2. Folklore—Norway.] I. Asbjørnsen, Peter Christen, 1812-1885. Tre bukkene Bruse. II. Title.
PZ8.C876Ro 2014
398.2—dc23
[E]
2012006585

Over the hills and through the hollows, three rowdy rockers—Billy Lee, Billy Joe, and Billy Bob—were rollin' to a gig at Nanny May's Shimmy Shack.

To reach the shack, the billies had to cross a bridge.
And the troll under that bridge? Man, was he a square.
Billy Lee roared up first.

Zug zugga Vroom zoom!

"Hey, daddy-o!" said the little billy.

"Rowdy kid!" snarled the troll. "Yer raisin' a ruckus and scarin' off my supper!"

“I’m cruisin’ to the Shimmy Shack to wail on my guitar.”

“No go, billy boy!” said the troll. “I’ll stomp yer geetar to smithereens!”

“Oh no, daddy-o! My guitar makes the twang so the crowd can do its thang.”

Billy Lee snatched his guitar and started a-wailin’.

zun,
zunna,
zow,
wow!

Right then, who should roar up? Billy Joe.

“Easy, big greasy!” said the medium-sized billy.

“Yer raisin’ a ruckus and scarin’ off my supper!” bellowed the troll.

"I'm cruisin' to the Shimmy Shack to slap on my bass."

"No go, billy boy!" said the troll. "I'll stomp yer bass to smithereens!"

“Hold that boot, coot! My bass makes the bump so the crowd can jump.”

Billy Joe took out his bass and started a-slappin’.

DOONG,
DOONGA,
DOONG,
DOWNG,
DOWNG!
ZUN,
ZUNNA,
ZOW,
WOW!

Right then, who should roar up?

Billy Bob.

"What's buzzin', cousin?" said the big-brother billy.

"Yer scarin' off my supper!" thundered the hungry troll.

"I'm just cruisin' to the Shimmy Shack to bang my buckets."

"No go, billy boy!" said the troll. "I'll stomp yer buckets to smithereens!"

"Freeze right there, square!
My drums make the beat so the
crowd moves its feet." Billy Bob
whipped out his drums and
started a-bangin'.

RAP, TAP, BOOMITY,
BOOM, BANG!
DOONG, DOONGA, DOONG,
DOWNG, DANG!
ZUN, ZUNNA, ZOW,
ZANG!

"I can't stand no more!" screamed the troll.

He charged, and . . .

WHAM-O! Billy Bob threw him head over britches smack into the back of his truck.

All three Rockabillies burned rubber to the Shimmy Shack.

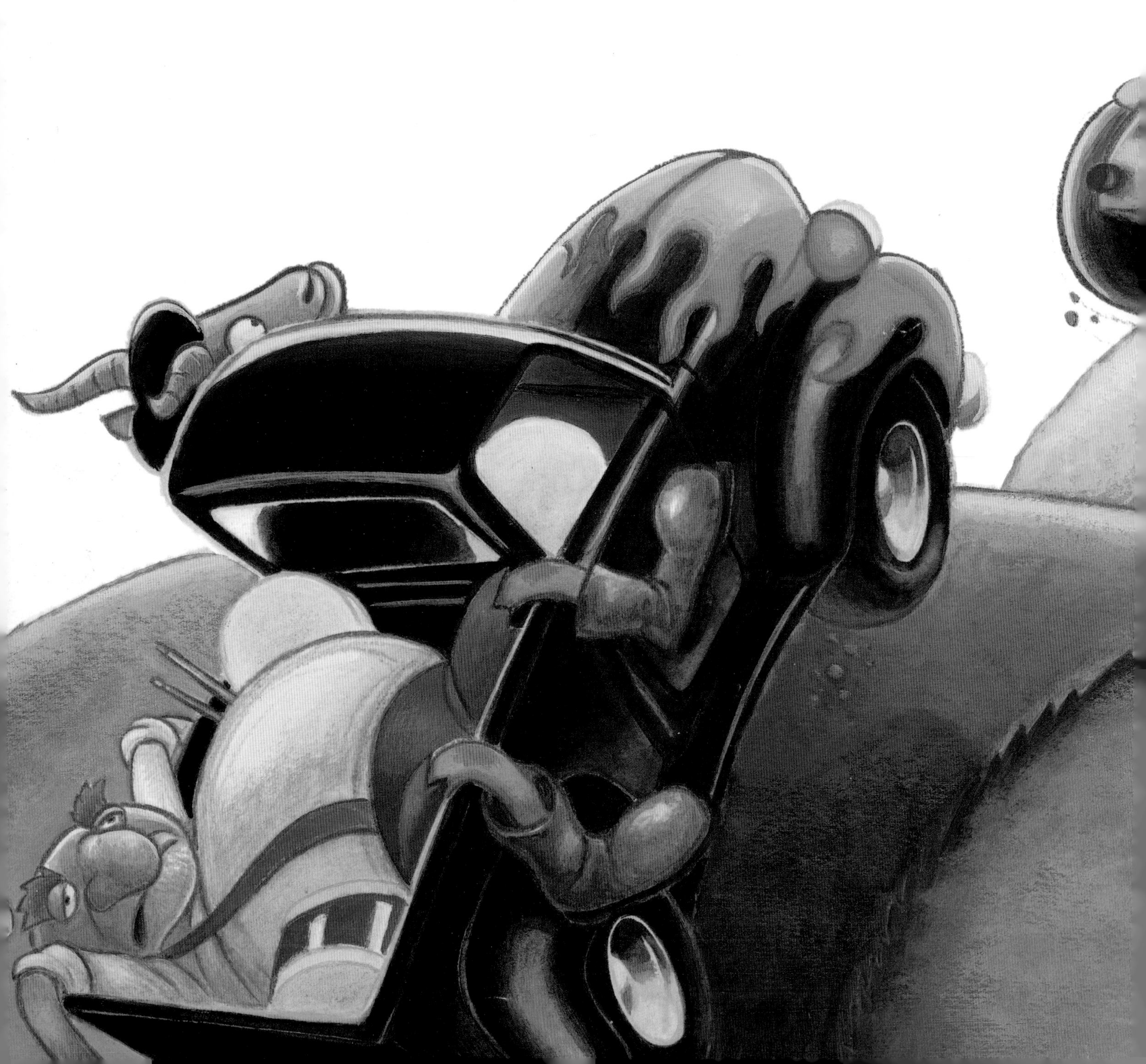

virrrrrrrr
Zug zugga vroom
zoom zoom zoom!

Nanny May brought the troll a heapin' helpin' of her rib-stickin' barbecue.

He sniffed. He grunted. He growled. He gobbled down the barbecue and grinned! "Let's raise a ruckus!" he hooted.

The Rockabilly Goats with their rockabilly knack
Hauled the cranky ol' troll to the rockin' Shimmy Shack,
Where the barbecue kept comin' till the troll ate his fill

And the rockin', rollin' billies let their rockabilly spill.
Then the troll was a-trompin' and a-stompin' his feet,
Movin' and a-groovin'
to the rockabilly beat.

From that night on, the troll rocked and rolled at every Rockabilly gig.

And he never missed supper again.